GONDRA'S
TREASURE

GONDRA'S TREASURE

Linda Sue Park

Illustrated by
Jennifer Black Reinhardt

CLARION BOOKS
Houghton Mifflin Harcourt
Boston   New York

With thanks to author Carole Wilkinson,
whose talk in 2012 first gave me
the idea for this story

— L.S.P.

CLARION BOOKS
3 Park Avenue, New York, New York 10016

Text copyright © 2019 by Linda Sue Park
Illustrations copyright © 2019 by Jennifer Black Reinhardt

Clarion Books is an imprint of
Houghton Mifflin Harcourt Publishing Company.

HMHCO.COM

The illustrations in the book were done in ink, watercolor, and collage paper.
The text was set in Aunt Mildred MVB.

Library of Congress Cataloging-in-Publication Data
Names: Park, Linda Sue, author. | Reinhardt, Jennifer Black, 1963–illustrator.
Title: Gondra's treasure / Linda Sue Park ; illustrated by Jennifer Black Reinhardt.
Description: Boston ; New York : Clarion Books, Houghton Mifflin Harcourt, [2019]
Summary: Gondra, a little dragon, celebrates her uniqueness while talking with her
parents about differences between her father's homeland in the East, and her
mother's in the West.
Identifiers: LCCN 2018032039 | ISBN 9780544546691 (hardback)
Subjects: | CYAC: Dragons—Fiction. | Individuality—Fiction. | Parent and child—Fiction.
BISAC: JUVENILE FICTION / Animals / Mythical. | JUVENILE FICTION / Family / Parents.
JUVENILE FICTION / Fantasy & Magic.
Classification: LCC PZ7.P22115 Gon 2019 | DDC [E]—dc23
LC record available at https://lccn.loc.gov/2018032039

Manufactured in China | SCP 10 9 8 7 6 5 4 3 2 1 | 4500744790

To the newest member
of my gloriously
mixed family,
Tia Dobbin
—L.S.P.

To my dad, C.O.B.,
and my mom,
R.M.B., thanks for
making me ME.
Love you.
—J.B.R.

My mom's family comes from the West.
Dad's family is from the East.
My name is Gondra, and I was born
somewhere in the middle.

"In the West, dragons breathe fire," Mom said.

"Isn't that dangerous?" I asked.

"That's what *I* said, when we first met," Dad said. "In the East, dragons breathe mist."

Mom shrugged. "Compared to fire, it seems . . . um . . .
pretty boring."

Dad frowned. "What did you say?"

Mom cleared her throat and spoke loudly. "I said 'pretty.'
Mist is pretty."

There's a picture of me when I was
a baby. A teeny tiny flame is coming
from one nostril and a wisp of mist
from the other.

"You were *adorable*," Mom said.

"The most beautiful baby
dragon ever," Dad agreed.

Now I can breathe fire *or* mist whenever I want.
Mist is great for hide-and-seek!

But I'm not allowed to breathe fire unless Dad or Mom is with me.

Both of my parents can fly. Mom has wings. Dad uses magic.
Whenever I ask Mom to go faster, she always says
the same thing.
   "This is fast enough, sweetie. You don't want my wings
to get tired, do you?"

"That's the problem with wings," Dad says.

I have wings, like Mom. But I can't fly yet because they're too small.

I won't know if I have flying magic until I'm bigger.

When I grow up, if I have wings *and* flying magic,
I'll be the fastest in the family!

Dad's scales are mostly blue and green.
He has a few red and gold ones too.
  "My side of the family has bronze scales,"
Mom said. "It's classier. Not as garish."
  "What does *garish* mean?" I asked.
  "Gaudy. Flashy."
  "Nothing wrong with a little flair," Dad said.

  "I like flashy," I said. "I like classy too."
  "Bronze, eh?" Dad said. "Well, whatever
color they are, they're gorgeous."
  Mom blushed. "Why, thank you, dear."

I'm mostly bronze, like Mom. But just the other day, I noticed that a few scales on my tail are starting to turn bluish green.

"Look at that!" Dad exclaimed. "Just like your dear old dad!"

He was so excited that he made huge clouds of mist, and it started raining in the living room.

Mom's ancestors lived in caves full of treasure.

"What did they want with all that stuff?" Dad asked.

"It was *treasure*, for heaven's sake," Mom said.

"Dad, everybody likes treasure!"

Some of Dad's family lived in lakes or rivers. The rest lived in the clouds.

"Our treasure was a magic pearl that we could hold in one claw," Dad said.

"Just one treasure?" I asked.

"What, were you too lazy to search for more?" Mom teased.

"Why have more than you need?" Dad said.

Mom's family sometimes had to fight humans to protect their treasure.

Dad's family used the magic pearl to control the weather. They provided rain when humans needed it. And when they were angry, they could send floods.

"I don't want to fight humans," I said.
"Or drown them. I want them to like me."

"Where I come from, humans *love* dragons," Dad said
proudly. "They make boats in the shape of dragons.
Sometimes they dress up as dragons and dance in parades."

Mom sighed. "I'm sorry to say that in the West, humans haven't always loved dragons. But they do love stories about us."

Living in a cave with treasure sounds like fun.
So does living in the clouds and making
it rain with a magic pearl.

"Mom? Dad? How come we don't live
in a cave anymore? Or in the clouds?"

"Times change," Mom said. "Things aren't the same as they used to be."

"Besides, don't you like our house?" Dad asked.

"Of course I do, but what happened to the magic pearl? And all the treasure?"

"Again?" Mom rolled her eyes. "You've asked us that a million times."

"We've told you before, remember?" Dad said.

"Oh, that's right. We don't need them anymore—because *I'm* your treasure."

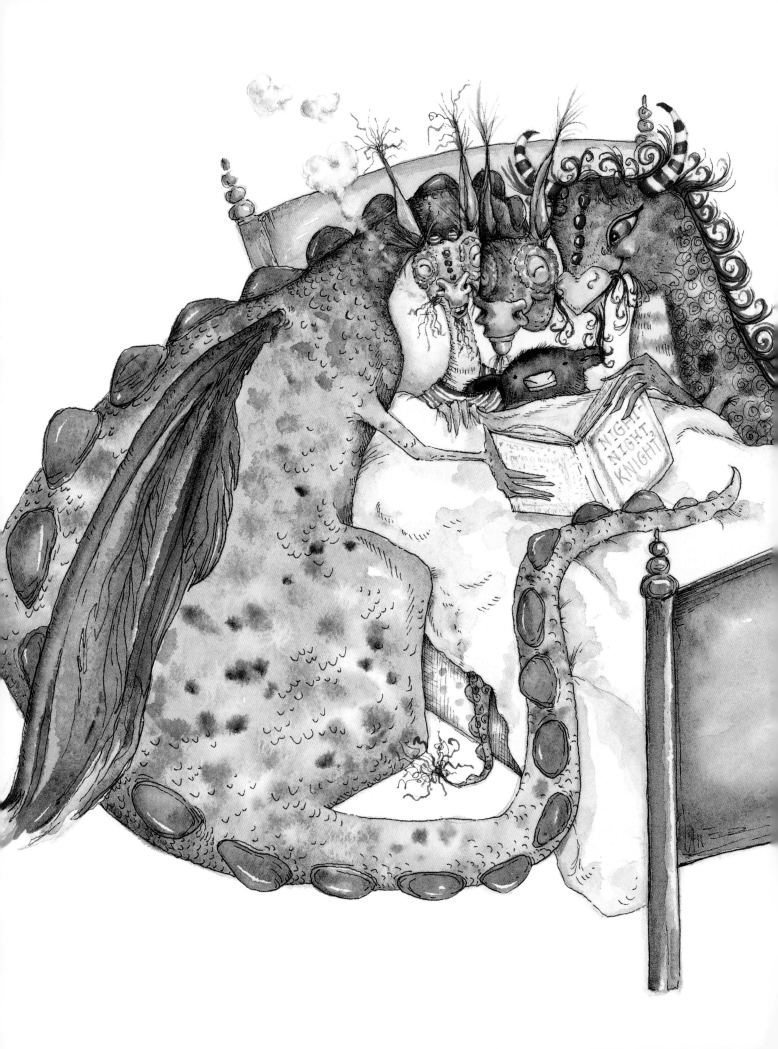

"The best treasure ever!" Dad said.
Mom smiled. "Why have more than you need?"

Author's Note

The story of Gondra's family shows some of the differences between Eastern and Western dragons. There are surprising similarities as well. Both are huge creatures with reptilian or snakelike bodies, magical powers, and a complex relationship with humans. How did people on opposite sides of the world come up with imaginary beings that share so many characteristics?

Some cultural anthropologists theorize that dragon myths arose when people unearthed fossilized dinosaur skeletons, which have been found on all seven of Earth's continents. I can easily imagine how the discovery of such gigantic bones would have given rise to fantastic stories.

The earliest known depiction of a dragon was found in China and is thought to be about seven thousand years old. Most if not all Asian dragons are probably derived from the Chinese dragon, *lóng* in Mandarin. Perhaps not surprisingly, China has some of the richest dinosaur fossil beds in the world.

In the Western or European tradition, dragons or dragon-like creatures are portrayed on Greek artifacts dating from 500 B.C. Earlier still (approximately 800 B.C.) are reliefs of the Sumerian *kur*, a fire-breathing serpentine creature. The Babylonian *Tiamat* from around the same time was, according to some scholars, a sea goddess who occasionally took the form of a dragon.

Humans evolved as prey: We are naturally fascinated by predators. Many species of monkeys throughout the world are preyed upon by snakes. If, as most scientists believe, we evolved from earlier primates, could a healthy respect for snakes be coded in our genes? And could this sense of awe be part of the reason why our ancestors told stories about magical snakelike creatures?

We might never discover the definitive answer to those questions. But I love the thought that no matter where we live or come from, we share similar fascinations, fears, and fantasies.